CLYDE:
THE CAT THAT CAME IN FROM THE COLD

TO MY FATHER,
WHO INSPIRED ME TO PURSUE MY DREAM,
AND TO MY HUSBAND AND DAUGHTER,
FOR THEIR ENCOURAGEMENT,
AND TO "CLYDE,"
FOR WITHOUT HIM THERE WOULD BE NO STORY.

THIS BOOK MAY BE ORDERED IN BULK,
DISCOUNT PRICING AVAILABLE
FOR RETAIL STORES, SCHOOLS, AND
NON-PROFIT ORGANIZATIONS.

CONTACT PUBLISHER AT
WWW.ZGIRLSPRESS.COM

PUBLISHED BY Z GIRLS PRESS
WWW.ZGIRLSPRESS.COM
SACRAMENTO, CALIFORNIA

FIRST EDITION PUBLISHED OCTOBER 6TH
COPYRIGHT 2018 DAPHNE STAMMER
SACRAMENTO, CALIFORNIA

DAPHNE STAMMER PHOTO CREDIT: DOROTHY CHAMPION

HARDBACK ISBN-13:978-0-9965683-9-5
PAPERBACK ISBN-13: 978-1-7328293-2-9
EBOOK ISBN-13: 978-1-7328293-0-5

CLYDE

THE CAT
THAT CAME IN FROM THE COLD
A TRUE STORY

STORY AND ILLUSTRATIONS BY
DAPHNE STAMMER

CLYDE WAS JUST A PLAIN, ORDINARY CAT. HE WAS NOT REALLY VERY HANDSOME. IN FACT, HE WAS SCRUFFY AND SKINNY. BUT HE HAD A DREAM.

HIS DREAM WAS TO BE A HOUSECAT. A HOUSECAT IS SPECIAL. AND SPOILED. AND LOVED.

THIS IS THE STORY OF CLYDE AND HIS SEARCH FOR HIS DREAM. HE WANDERED FAR AND NEAR LOOKING FOR A PLEASANT HOME. HIS SEARCH TOOK HIM THROUGH OLD BROKEN-DOWN BUILDINGS AND LONG SCARY ALLEYS.

CLYDE DID NOT HAVE A HOME. HE HAD TO HUNT FOR HIS FOOD. HE HAD TO SLEEP IN THE BUSHES. BUT HE WOULD NOT GIVE UP HIS DREAM.

AFTER MANY DAYS AND WEEKS, HE CAME UPON A VERY NICE NEIGHBORHOOD. HERE HE MET FRIENDLY, FAT CATS AND KIND, PLEASANT PEOPLE.

CLYDE THOUGHT THIS WOULD BE A GOOD PLACE
TO FIND THE PERFECT FAMILY WHO WOULD LOVE HIM.
HE FOUND A PRETTY YELLOW HOUSE. IT BELONGED
TO THE KITTENBERGS AND THEY LOVED CATS.
THEY ALREADY HAD THREE!

ONE DAY THERE WERE FOUR BOWLS ON THE FRONT PORCH. HE THOUGHT MAYBE ONE OF THE BOWLS COULD BE FOR HIM. AND IT WAS. THE MEALS TASTED SO GOOD!

BUT CLYDE KNEW THAT IF HIS DREAM OF BECOMING A HOUSECAT WAS TO COME TRUE, HE WOULD HAVE TO WORK VERY HARD.

HE WOULD GUARD THE HOUSE.

HE WOULD CHASE AWAY STRAY DOGS AND CATS.

HE WOULD KEEP THE MICE AWAY.

...AND HE WOULD WATCH THE GARDEN GROW.

THEN WINTER CAME. IT WAS VERY COLD AND WET. THE COLD WIND BLEW ALMOST EVERY DAY. CLYDE SAT LOOKING IN THE WINDOW. IT LOOKED SO WARM INSIDE! HE SAT THERE HOPING THE FAMILY WOULD LET HIM COME IN.

AND THEN IT HAPPENED! MRS. KITTENBERG OPENED THE DOOR AND CALLED TO HIM! HIS DREAM WAS COMING TRUE! HE RAN INTO THE HOUSE!

SHE MADE HIM A SPECIAL BED.

HE HAD HIS VERY OWN LITTERBOX.

AND HE GOT TO EAT WHENEVER HE WANTED.

ON SHOPPING DAY HE LOVED TO PLAY IN THE GROCERY BAGS.

SOME DAYS THE ONLY WAY HE COULD
EXPRESS HIS JOY WAS BY CHASING HIS TAIL
AROUND THE ROOM!

MRS. KITTENBERG LOVED HIM VERY MUCH. HE LIKED TO SIT WITH HER WHILE SHE WATCHED TELEVISION.

WHEN THE DAYS GOT WARMER, CLYDE WOULD FOLLOW THE SUN THROUGHOUT THE DAY, GOING FROM ROOM TO ROOM, CURLING UP IN ITS WARMTH.

HE WAS SO HAPPY!

CLYDE'S DREAM HAD FINALLY COME TRUE. HE WAS NOT JUST AN ORDINARY CAT. HE WAS THE CAT THAT CAME IN FROM THE COLD.

HE WAS A HOUSECAT!

Made in the USA
San Bernardino, CA
26 November 2018